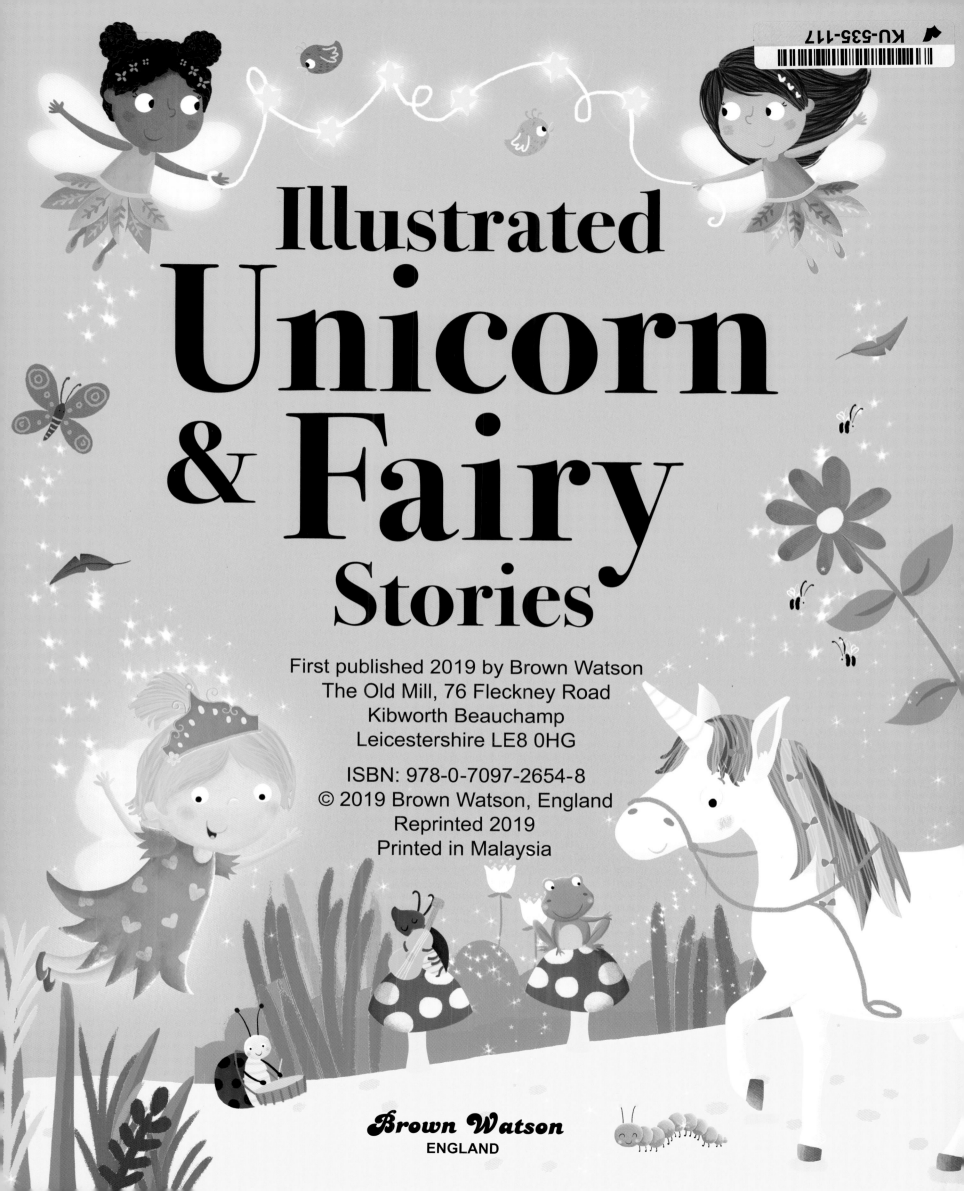

Illustrated Unicorn & Fairy Stories

First published 2019 by Brown Watson
The Old Mill, 76 Fleckney Road
Kibworth Beauchamp
Leicestershire LE8 0HG

ISBN: 978-0-7097-2654-8
© 2019 Brown Watson, England
Reprinted 2019
Printed in Malaysia

Brown Watson
ENGLAND

Contents

Make a Wish

It was Princess Phoebe's birthday. "Where are my presents?" she cried. Her dad laughed. "Happy Birthday, Phoebe! Your present was too big to wrap. He's in the garden." She rushed outside and there was a fabulous white unicorn. "Thanks Dad," she said beaming.

"Your name is Theo," she told her unicorn. "I've always wished for a unicorn and now I have you. I have lots of wishes. Sometimes I wish I had a little puppy... Oh!" she exclaimed. "Just like this one!"

"There are other things on my wish list," she told Theo. "For instance, I'd love to sit on a magic carpet with an Arabian prince and we'd eat cake together... Oh!" she exclaimed, for suddenly her wish came true.

"That cake was yummy!" said Phoebe when the prince had gone. It was a warm day and Phoebe got hot riding along. "Sometimes I wish I lived in a cold country. Then I'd go skiing every day... Oh!" Suddenly there she was in the snow skiing with her friends.

"That was such fun," she said when her wish had faded. It was getting late now and the evening star was twinkling in the sky. "Look, Theo! Don't you just wish you could fly right next to the stars?" Suddenly there they were, each star more magnificent than the last.

That evening, the king asked her, "Did you have a lovely ride today? They say unicorns have magic powers to grant your every wish. Imagine how funny that would be," he chuckled. Phoebe laughed too. If only he knew!

Snow Adventure

"Where are you going to take us today, Pearl?" Princess Harriet asked her unicorn. "Lady and Pearl love to give us an adventure, don't they?" said Princess Annabelle. At the top of the mountain they stopped and looked at each other excitedly. "Ready to fly?" said Annabelle. "Let's GO!!"

Both unicorns took off and suddenly the princesses were high up in the sky, flying over a rainbow and through the clouds. The villages and people looked tiny below them. Some time later, the unicorns came down to land. "Brrr... it's cold," said Harriet.

"You'll soon warm up," said Annabelle, pointing to their new, snuggly outfits. "Great!" said Harriet. "Let's go skating!" They sped through the ice and twirled like dancers. "I'm thirsty," said Annabelle. "Let's go and get something to drink."

Soon they arrived at an ice palace. Inside, a queen was sitting on the throne and she called out to them in a demanding voice, "Girls! Girls! Haven't you finished building my igloo yet?" They looked at each other and stifled a giggle. An igloo?

But they stopped laughing when the queen insisted they made her an igloo. "This is hard work," complained Harriet as she lifted each large block of ice. At last it was completed and the queen gave them a mug of steaming hot chocolate. "The best ever," sighed Annabelle.

All too soon their adventure was over. When they were getting ready for bed, Harriet placed something in Annabelle's hand. It was a recipe card for the hot chocolate. "Where did you...?"

"The queen gave it to me," said Harriet.

"Maybe she wasn't so bad after all!" laughed Annabelle.

The Laughing Princess

Jasmine, Daisy and Matilda lived in the grounds of a beautiful palace. "Have you ever seen the princess?" asked Jasmine one day.

"Only once," said Daisy. "She is the most beautiful princess in the world."

"I wish I could meet her," said Jasmine. "I'm going to explore the gardens until I find her."
"Well, be careful," said Daisy. "And beware of grumpy Greta." But Jasmine had flown off. "Have you seen the princess?" she asked a frog. "Yes, she went over the bridge," he said.

Jasmine flew quickly over the bridge. She was so excited she forgot Daisy's warning. "Hello," said Greta. "Looking for someone?"

"Yes," said Jasmine. "The princess."

Greta nodded in the direction of the maze.

"Over there," she said with a glint in her eye.

The hedges were too tall for Jasmine to fly over. She followed one path and then another. But she kept coming to a dead end. "I'm lost!" she cried. "Now I'll never see the princess." Eventually she found a way out but was so tired she fell asleep on the nearest flower.

Two voices woke her up. "Hello Jasmine," said Matilda. "We thought you might want some help. Have you seen the princess yet?"

"No," said Jasmine. "But it will be more fun looking for her together."

"What pretty gardens!" said Matilda. "Not as pretty as the princess," sighed Jasmine, when at last they found her. The princess laughed and the three fairies joined in which sent a ripple of laughter all across the land.

The Grumpy Princess

Most of the time, Princess Grace enjoyed being a princess. But one day she woke up very grumpy. "I HATE wearing a tiara," she said and threw it across the room. "And I HATE wearing dresses all the time!" She stomped out of the room and into the garden.

Her friend Lily the stable girl was outside, brushing her horse. "What's wrong?" she asked Grace when she saw her face.

"Humph," sighed Grace. "I'm fed up with being a princess. I just want to be ordinary for once."

Lily thought for a moment. "I know!" she said. "Let's swap for the day. You can wear my clothes and I can wear yours! And we'll do some fun things together." "I'd like that," said Grace cheering up. "And as a special treat you can ride Unicorn."

It was such fun to start with. They went to the zoo and laughed at the monkeys. They went to the seaside and paddled in the sea. Grace liked the feel of the sand between her toes. "I'm starving," she said. "Race you to the snack van."

But by the afternoon, Grace was grumpy again. Everywhere they went people curtseyed at Lily and threw her flowers. But they didn't even look at Grace. They thought she was just a stable girl. "STOP!" she shouted suddenly. "She's not the princess! I AM!"

"But I thought you wanted to be ordinary," said Lily.
"I did," sighed Grace. "But I was jealous when everyone admired you and not me."
"Next time we could both wear stable clothes," suggested Lily. "Or we could both wear princess dresses," said Grace. "Perfect!" said Lily and they smiled at each other.

To the Rescue

Deep in the Great Forest, Ellie the unicorn was playing hide and seek with Dusty the dragon. "You'll never find me," said Dusty, which wasn't quite true as often his tail gave him away. But they always had fun together.

They had run away to the forest to escape evil King Henry, who had locked the real king in the dungeon and taken his place. "I don't want any fairy book nonsense in my kingdom," Henry had said. "Away with dragons, unicorns and knights!"

One day, a knight came galloping into the forest. "What are you doing here?" he asked Dusty and Ellie. "I didn't think there were any unicorns or dragons alive still." "There aren't," said Ellie. "I'm just an old donkey and he's an overgrown lizard."

William the knight laughed. "What nonsense! You must have been in this forest so long you've forgotten who you are. But look, we haven't got a lot of time. Henry is after me and I need your help to stop his plans once and for all."

After a lot of persuading Dusty and Ellie agreed. "I'll teach you a few skills you seem to have lost," said William. All day William got them running and jumping until finally they could both fly again! When it got dark they went to the castle to carry out William's plan.

Dusty swooped down, picked Henry up and suspended him over the lake. "HELP!" cried Henry. "Let me go!" So Dusty dropped him into the water. Meanwhile, Ellie rammed down the dungeon door and the real king ran out overjoyed. "HURRAY!" cried the people. "The king is free!"

The Bossy Fairy

Four fairy sisters lived in Fairy Cottage in Fairyland. Imogen was the eldest. She liked to boss her sisters around. "Chloe! Come and clean the windows. Alice! Come and polish the toadstools. Willow! Get me a berry juice, please."

Her sisters started to get fed up with her. "We never get any time to ourselves these days," said Chloe. "And she doesn't do a thing to help!" added Alice. But Willow sat thinking.

"I think I have the answer," said Willow. "We can send her on a holiday to her aunt's house. She won't forget that one in a hurry," she chuckled. The others were intrigued.

"A holiday!" said Imogen. "What a lovely idea. I'll pack my bags right away." When it was time to go she waved goodbye and flew off. "I think I might finish sewing my cushion," said Alice. Chloe practised her dancing and Willow did a painting. They had a lovely time!

Meanwhile Imogen arrived at her aunt's house. "Come in," said Aunt Millie. "I'm so glad you're here to give a helping hand." Every day, Imogen had lots of jobs to do – dusting, washing and ironing. "Some holiday!" thought Imogen as she collapsed into bed at night.

At the end of the week Imogen came home. "Aunt Millie worked me hard and bossed me about. But then I realised that's exactly what I'd been doing to you. I'm sorry. I'll try and be kinder from now on." And she was – so everyone was happy again.

Stolen!

One day a messenger ran into the Royal Dining Room. "Your Majesty! Someone has broken into the Royal Treasury and stolen all the gold coins."

"What a disaster!" said the King. "What are we going to do?"

"We could sell all my dresses," said Princess Amelia.
"Whoever heard of a princess without dresses?" said the King.
"We could give cook a rest and eat fruit instead of cake."
"What, no cake?" said the King.

"Well... we could charge people to ride Snowflake," said Princess Amelia. Children came from miles around to ride the beautiful white unicorn. But now Princess Amelia only had time to ride her at night.

In the woods, two robbers were counting out the gold
coins they had stolen. But a dragon ran out and chased
them away. "Chocolate coins," he said,
licking his lips. "My favourite." He took a bite then spat
it out. "This chocolate's hard! I'm sending it back."

At the palace, things weren't going too well. Snowflake was tired of giving rides, the King was fed up of eating bananas and Princess Amelia was disappointed she had earned so little. But one day there was a knock at the door. "I'll go," said the King.

There was no one there but there was a large sack on the doorstep and a note. This chocolate is hard. Please send a new batch. The Dragon. "Cook!" shouted the King. "Prepare a feast! We're rich again! Oh... and order a year's worth of the finest chocolate and deliver it to the Dragon's Den, please."

Musical Fairies

Penny loved to sing. She sang as she cooked, she sang around the garden and she even sang herself to sleep. She was very shy though and didn't like others listening to her singing. "But you have such a beautiful voice," said Megan and Iris, her best friends.

One day Megan suggested they have a musical evening and invite all the woodland fairies to come and listen. "I can play the flute, Iris can play the sax and Penny, you can sing."

"Oh," said Penny in a small voice. "I'm too shy to sing."

"Alright," said Megan. "I'll do the singing then... even though your voice is prettier than mine."

"Can we join your band?" asked the ladybirds.

"That would be lovely!" said Iris. They all practised hard together and it started to sound good.

"It's time to give out the invitations," said Megan. Penny was nervous. She had to give one to Katie who was loud and boisterous. "A musical evening! How lovely," said Katie. "Can I bring my four sisters?" But timid Penny had already flown away.

The day of the musical evening arrived. But something was wrong. "My throat is sore," whispered Megan. "I don't think I can sing tonight." Even the berry juice didn't make her better. "Please sing for me instead, Penny," croaked Megan.

Penny was afraid – but she didn't want to let her friends down. "OK then," she said. She took a deep breath and sang the first note. Then an amazing thing happened. The audience smiled at her and sang along too! All her fears vanished and she enjoyed every minute.

Rosie's Big Decision

It was the day of the Royal Ball and Princess Rosie was trying to decide what to wear. "Pink or blue?" she asked the Queen. "Blue," said the Queen. "It brings out the colour of your eyes so well."

Just then the King came into her room. "Have you decided on your ballgown?" he asked. "Dad – which do you prefer? Pink or blue?"

"Hmm...." he stroked his chin. "Pink is my favourite."

"After all we didn't call you Rosie for nothing!"

Rosie still couldn't decide so she went into the garden. She sang a little song to herself: "Blue or pink, pink or blue; what is a princess going to do?"

April the unicorn was listening in. "I like blue myself," she said.

Rosie sat down on a log and carried on singing, "Pink or blue, blue or pink? Hey, little fairy what do you think?" "Pink!" said the fairy, doing a little twirl. "I love the colour of roses, foxgloves and peonies."

Rosie carried on singing: "Blue or pink, pink or blue; a dress, a sash and handbag too!"
Just then Prince Sebastian arrived. "I've brought you a present," he said. "I hope you like it."

Rosie carefully undid the wrapping and opened the box. Inside was the most beautiful pair of shoes she had ever seen. They had swirls of beads, a tiny bow and a dainty heel. "I LOVE them!" said Rosie. "I'm definitely wearing pink to the ball now," she added smiling.

The Birthday Party

Princess Evie was very excited. She was going to Princess Cara's birthday party at the Castle. Her dad kissed her goodbye as she climbed into the coach. "Have you got the present?" he asked.

"Yes, Dad," she said.

When she arrived there were lots of other princesses there. "Come and see Cara open her presents," said Princess Florence.

"Ooo, look what Evie's given me!" said Cara. "A lovely unicorn with a brush so I can comb its mane and tail!"

"We're going to play hide and seek next," said Cara. "The castle is so big there are plenty of places to hide. I'll close my eyes first and count to ten." Evie had never been to a castle before but she was good at hiding. Her first hiding place was behind the staircase.

"We thought we'd never find you," said Florence some
time later. Where could Evie hide next? She hurried
down one corridor and then the next. She could hear
footsteps getting closer so she quickly opened the
nearest door and went inside.

She was very surprised to see Cara's mum with her new baby. "I'm really sorry," said Evie. "I got lost playing hide and seek."

"That's alright," said Cara's mum kindly. "Would you like to see the baby?"

"Yes please!" said Evie. She adored babies.

Suddenly, Cara burst into the room. "Come on!" she said. "We're going to have fireworks now." Evie kissed the tiny baby fingers goodbye and skipped outside with the others. "I've had a wonderful time," said Evie. "So have I," said Cara and gave her friend a big squeeze.

Goodbye!